I0692500

Hablot Knight Browne, Frederic George Kitton

A Memoir

With a selection from his correspondence by Fred. G. Kitton

Hablot Knight Browne, Frederic George Kitton

A Memoir
With a selection from his correspondence by Fred. G. Kitton

ISBN/EAN: 9783337146191

Printed in Europe, USA, Canada, Australia, Japan

Cover: Foto ©Raphael Reischuk / pixelio.de

More available books at **www.hansebooks.com**

"PHIZ"

(HABLOT KNIGHT BROWNE)

A Memoir.

INCLUDING

A Selection from his Correspondence and Notes on his Principal Works.

BY

FRED. G. KITTON.

WITH A PORTRAIT, AND NUMEROUS ILLUSTRATIONS.

LONDON :

W. SATCHELL & CO.,

19, TAVISTOCK STREET COVENT GARDEN.

MDCCCLXXXII.

LONDON :
G. NORMAN AND SON, PRINTERS, HART STREET,
COVENT GARDEN.

PREFACE.

TAKING into consideration the ability of the Artist whose name has become identified with the works of DICKENS, of LEVER, and of AINSWORTH; and who has contributed in the course of the present century more largely (perhaps with the single exception of CRUIKSHANK) to the embellishment of popular books than any other known illustrator; it would seem an inexcusable omission, almost amounting to neglect, if the life and labours of the late HABLOT KNIGHT BROWNE met with no more worthy recognition than the fleeting comments of the daily press.

Such, at least, is my opinion; and as a humble tribute to the memory of an able and industrious draughtsman, and fertile designer, I place on record the more generally interesting particulars of an honourable and exemplary career.

To Mr. W. G. BROWNE and Dr. EDGAR BROWNE, sons of the deceased artist, my best thanks are due for a kindly interest in my work, manifested more especially by the loan of many interesting letters dashed off on various occasions by "Phiz" in the wildest spirit of fun; and a willing consent to their appearance in print.

I have also to acknowledge the courtesy of Messrs. H. SOTHERAN & Co., for permission to copy for publication a few letters written by "Phiz" to CHARLES DICKENS, which are now published for the first time. For the Portrait (copied from a photograph, perhaps the best of the very few now in existence) I am indebted to the Proprietors of *The Graphic.*

And lastly, the Author desires to associate with this *brochure* the name of his friend, Mr. GEORGE REDWAY, who has rendered much valuable assistance in bringing it before the public.

FRED. G. KITTON.

25, PAULTONS SQUARE,
                      CHELSEA, S.W.
   August, 1882.

LIST OF PLATES.

NOTE.—With the exception of the Portrait, and the "Dombey fancies," the above engravings are printed from electro-types of the original blocks, which were first published in *Master Humphrey's Clock* (1840-1).

"PHIZ" (H. K. BROWNE) A MEMOIR.

"Fizz, Whizz, or something of that sort," humorous Tom Hood would say, when trying to recall the pseudonym that has since become so familiar by means of the innumerable works of art to which it was appended. At the time Hablot* Knight Browne first used this quaint *soubriquet*, it was customary to look upon book-illustrators as second, or even third-rate artists—mere hacks in fact; and for this reason they usually suppressed their real names, in order to give themselves the opportunity of earning the title of *artist*, when producing more ambitious results as painters. Occasionally, whether by accident or design, the subject of this memoir would affix his real name to his illustrations; and the public were consequently under the impression that the two signatures were those of different artists, and were even wont to remark that "*Browne's work was better than that of 'Phiz!'*"

It is not, perhaps, generally known that the artist's first *nom de crayon* was "Nemo," which to some extent bears out the above statement that a book-illustrator was considered a "nobody." Mr. Browne himself, in referring to the *Pickwick Papers*, gave the following explanation:—"I think I signed myself as 'Nemo' to my first etchings (those of No. 4) before adopting 'Phiz' as my *soubriquet*, to harmonize—I suppose—better with Dickens' 'Boz.'" It is only on the earliest printed plates in some copies of the *Pickwick Papers* that the signature of "Nemo" can be faintly traced.

Hablot Knight Browne, son of William Loder Browne, a descendant from a Norfolk family, was born on the 12th of July, 1815, at Kennington, London. He was educated at a private school in Norfolk, and from an early age

---

* Pronounced *Hab-lo*, after a Monsieur Hablot, a captain in the French army, and a friend of the family.

evinced a taste for drawing, which, being recognized by his relatives, induced them to apprentice him to FINDEN, the well-known line-engraver. An anecdote is told of him during his apprenticeship which will bear repetition. Finding BROWNE very painstaking and conscientious, his master usually sent him with engraved plates to the printer, in order that he might superintend the operation of proof-taking. As printers usually take their own time over such matters, the youth found that this waiting the pressman's pleasure tried his patience too much. It therefore occurred to him that to spend the interval in the British Museum, hard by, would be much more suited to his tastes. On his returning with the proofs, FINDEN would praise the boy's diligence, little thinking what trick had been practised on him.

Line-engraving, however, did not find much favour with the future "Phiz," the process being too tedious; for FINDEN would probably occupy some weeks to produce a small plate, which by the quicker process of etching, could have been executed in as many hours. He accordingly suspended operations in that quarter, and, in conjunction with a young kindred spirit, hired a small attic, and employed his time in the more fascinating pursuit of water-colour drawing, which he continued to follow with remark-able assiduity until a few days before his death.

These juvenile disciples of the brush then worked hard at drawing in colour. BROWNE paid his share of the rent in drawings, which he produced rapidly; indeed, there was a solemn compact between the co-workers to "do three a day"—they subsisting, meanwhile, on the simplest fare. At this time he attended the evening class at the "Life" School in St. Martin's Lane, and was a fellow-pupil with ETTY, the famous painter of the "nude." It was BROWNE's great delight to watch this talented student at work, and he considerably neglected his own studies in consequence.

At the age of seventeen, or thereabouts, he succeeded in gaining a medal offered for competition by the Society of Arts for the best representation of an historical subject; and was again fortunate in obtaining a prize, from the same Society, for a large etching of "John Gilpin." Mr. GEORGE AUGUSTUS SALA, himself an artist of no small ability, remembers to have seen, in a shop-window in Wardour Street, a certain print by a young man named HABLOT BROWNE, representing the involuntary flight of

John Gilpin, scattering the pigs and poultry in his never-to-be-forgotten ride.

By the time he had attained his twentieth year he had acquired considerable facility with the pencil. CHARLES DICKENS, but three years his senior, and with whom the name of "Phiz" is inseparably connected, had just then made a wonderful reputation by his "Sketches," which first appeared, at intervals, during 1834-5, and were afterwards published in book form, illustrated by the renowned GEORGE CRUIKSHANK.

In 1836, there appeared in print a pamphlet of some forty or fifty pages, entitled *Sunday under Three Heads— As it is; as Sabbath Bills would make it; as it might be made;* "By Timothy Sparks; illustrated by H. K. B.;" and dedicated to the Bishop of London. The author was CHARLES DICKENS, whose satire was levelled at Sir Andrew Agnew and the extreme Sabbatarian party, and had immediate reference to a bill "for the better observance of the Sabbath," which the House of Commons had recently thrown out by a small majority. The illustrations in this little work were drawn by HABLOT BROWNE, and are very choice examples of wood-engraving of the school that existed half a century ago. Its original price was one shilling, but having become very scarce, it is now worth more than its weight in gold.

These early productions of BROWNE's pencil at once introduced him to public notice, and DICKENS showed his appreciation of their excellence by selecting him as the illustrator of the *Pickwick Papers*, which appeared during the early part of that year. It is well known to the readers of Forster's *Life of Dickens*, that the idea of "Pickwick" was suggested to the author by ROBERT SEYMOUR, whose tastes induced him to etch a few plates of sporting subjects to which DICKENS was to supply the text. Thus commenced that immortal work known as *The Posthumous Papers of the Pickwick Club.* SEYMOUR produced seven illustrations, when he committed suicide, which obliged the publishers to make arrangements with another artist. R. W. BUSS * succeeded SEYMOUR, and etched two plates, which DICKENS, who had by this time assumed the control

* It was BUSS who illustrated Mrs. Trollope's Serial Story, *The Widow Married,* which was published in *The New Monthly Magazine,* 1840.

of the work, thought so unsatisfactory (as indeed they were), that he declined his further services. Here a fresh opening was created, and WILLIAM MAKEPEACE THACKERAY competed with HABLOT KNIGHT BROWNE for the post; both submitting to DICKENS' inspection some specimens of their work.

The choice fell upon "Phiz," the artist whose ability has so admirably proved the wisdom of the selection; and THACKERAY thereupon determined to adopt another profession, with what happy results let *Esmond* testify. Who could say whether *Vanity Fair* would ever have been written had this mighty penman been chosen to succeed BUSS? It is curious to note THACKERAY's great anxiety to become an artist; he even went abroad to study, but SALA tells us that "Mr. THACKERAY drew, perhaps, rather worse than he had done before beginning his continental studies, although at that time he actually supplied a series of etchings to illustrate DOUGLAS JERROLD's *Men of Character*, which were prodigies of badness."

When "Phiz" had been selected as the illustrator of the *Pickwick Papers*, his generous rival was the first to tell him the good news, and offer his congratulations.

"Phiz" may now be said to have fairly commenced his career as a book-illustrator. His sense of humour corresponded so exactly with that of DICKENS, that a mere suggestion enabled him to vividly represent the scenes described by the author. It has been remarked (and truly) that in many cases the plates do not correspond with the text; but this can be accounted for. DICKENS, then an enthusiastic young author, and somewhat impetuous in his demands for drawings, would arrive unexpectedly at BROWNE's studio, hurriedly read a few pages of manuscript, and exclaiming, "Now, I want you to illustrate that," would take an abrupt departure, carrying the manuscript off with him. As soon as the artist could collect his faculties, he would try to recall the scene so hastily described, and endeavour to put it on paper. DICKENS himself, in his preface to the *Pickwick Papers*, gives a similar explanation, viz.—"It is due to the gentleman, whose designs accompany the letterpress, to state that the interval has been so short between the production of each number in manuscript and its appearance in print, that the greater portion of the illustrations have been executed by the artist from the author's verbal description of what he intended to write."

It is therefore not surprising that a few errors, in such details as the number of boys in a procession,* or the dress of an individual, should occur.

Of DICKENS' Novels, *Martin Chuzzlewit* contains, perhaps, our etcher's most vigorous productions, but the small wood-cut illustrations in *Master Humphrey's Clock* are very praiseworthy, and without doubt conduced greatly to the popularity of the book.

The illustrations in the *Pickwick Papers* are on the whole inferior to many which "Phiz" subsequently executed. But an exception must be made in favour of the artist's realization of the character of Sam Weller, than which, even SEYMOUR's happy invention of Mr. Pickwick did not more effectually ensure the popularity of DICKENS' comic epic and give it a "deathless date."

The extraordinary demand for copies of the *Pickwick Papers* necessitated a re-etching of the copper-plates, which, owing to friction caused by the printer's hand, had become very much worn. This reproduction will account for any slight difference in the details of the illustrations; for the repetition of subjects once etched, was a task by no means congenial to the artist; and this no doubt induced him to say, some years afterwards, in a letter to one of his sons, "O! I'm a' weary, I'm a' weary of this illustrating business."

Artists frequently experience great difficulty in realizing, to the author's satisfaction, the description of scenes and characters. An illustration is here given showing BROWNE's various "fancies for Mr. Dombey," all of which failed to please DICKENS, who also expressed his disapprobation of this artist's treatment of another subject in *Dombey and Son*. "I am really *distressed*," writes he, "by the illustration of Mrs. Pipchin and Paul. It is so frightfully and wildly wide of the mark. Good Heaven! in the commonest and most literal construction of the text, it is all wrong. She is described as an old lady, and Paul's 'miniature arm-chair' is mentioned more than once. He ought to be sitting in a little arm-chair down in the corner of the fire-place, staring up at her. I can't say what pain and vexation it is to be so utterly misrepresented. I would cheerfully have given a hundred pounds to have kept this illustration out of the book. He never could have got that idea of Mrs. Pipchin if he had attended to the text. Indeed, I

* See *Dombey and Son*, Vol. I, p. 113—"Doctor Blimber's Young Gentlemen."

think he does better without the text; for then the notion is made easy to him in short description, and he can't help taking it in."

As the tale proceeded, the artist more than compensated for his unsuccessful rendering of this incident; and with "Micawber," in *David Copperfield*, he obtained the author's entire approbation, who says, "Browne has sketched an uncommonly characteristic and capital Mr. Micawber for the next number." Again, with reference to an illustration in *Bleak House*, "Browne has done Skimpole, and helped to make him singularly unlike the great original."*

Of the private life of "Phiz" little is known. His extreme nervousness and dislike to publicity was often misconstrued as pride; and DICKENS even had considerable difficulty in occasionally persuading him to meet a few friends and spend a pleasant evening. When he did accept such invitations, he invariably tried to seclude himself in a corner of the room, or behind a curtain. His desire for a quiet, unobtrusive life, induced him to pass most of his time in country retirement, all business matters in town being transacted by an intimate friend.† Authors or publishers wishing to have a personal interview with "Phiz" were compelled to visit him at his residence, a few miles from town, and many were the *contretemps* on dark nights as they crossed a bleak moor to reach their destination. His sons looked forward to the time when visitors were expected, in order to hear the stories of wild adventure which generally befell them, and to laugh at their discomfiture.

"Phiz" had been from his boyhood accustomed to horses, and frequently hunted with the Surrey hounds. To this circumstance is due the extreme facility with which he delineated the horse in action in the hunting field and elsewhere. At one time he contributed sketches to *The Sporting Gazette*. This industrious artist was never known to take a lengthened holiday, but occasionally spent a few days at the seaside, where, no doubt, his pencil was fully employed. A letter, written while staying at Margate, to his son Mr. Walter G. Browne (whom, for some unknown reason he styled "Doctor"), shows his innate sense of humour.

---

* Leigh Hunt.
† Mr. R. Young, who also undertook the precarious task of "biting in" his plates.

Tuesday, June 19,
6A, CRESCENT PLACE, MARGATE.

MY DEAR DR.,

I hääve my W. C. White :*—but I have no white *collars*—and as I am swelling it about without a necktie—mine having mysteriously disappeared, left behind in a bath probably—perhaps it would be coming it too strong to appear without collars also, and it is hardly warm enough for it either. Your P.O. is from the Miscellany—to H. K. Browne—from Mr. Barrett—Xtian name unknown—and no matter. Any blocks that come, forward on. Send me a * * * * * * before I return. I did some very good shades myself— of myself—unconsciously—yesterday evening. The baths run along one side of the High Street, flush with the pavement—and I found when I had nearly finished my toilet that the gas-burner was so ingeniously placed, that it was impossible for any bather to avoid casting gigantic studies of the nude upon the window blind.—This sort of thing.—"

* * * * * *

[Here follow several other sketches of the bather in various attitudes].

His appreciation of fun is thus referred to by DICKENS in a letter to Mrs. Dickens, dating from the Lion Hotel, Shrewsbury. "Thursday, Nov. 1st, 1838.—We were at the play last night. It was a bespeak—'The Love Chase,' a ballet (with a phenomenon !), divers songs, and 'A Roland

* Water-colour white.

for an Oliver.' It is a good theatre, but the actors are very funny. Browne laughed with such indecent heartiness at one point of the entertainment, that an old gentleman in the next box suffered the most violent indignation."

In 1837, "Phiz" accompanied DICKENS to Flanders, for a ten days' summer holiday; and in 1838 they went to Yorkshire, a journey which resulted in the production of *Nicholas Nickleby*.

The following year he made one of a party of four, and visited, with DICKENS, MACREADY and FORSTER, nearly all the London prisons. These joint tours of Author and Artist could not fail to assist the realization of the scenes they intended to depict.

It is an interesting fact in connection with the career of "Phiz," that he would never agree to draw from the living model,—all his representations of moving crowds, and the various types of humanity, which his etchings exhibit, being drawn from recollection. He would sometimes make a few jottings in pencil—mere memoranda—when anything struck him as being worthy of reproduction, but beyond that he depended on his excellent memory. For example, he would go to Epsom on the Derby Day without taking a pencil even, and, on returning home, would draw to the life exact portraits of any conspicuous or eccentric character he had seen on the course.

As previously stated, BROWNE was extremely fond of water-colour drawing, and executed some thousands during his life; not unfrequently a day's work would be represented by three or four of these productions. They were not caricatures, as one might suppose, but rural scenes *à la Watteau*, and allegorical subjects. This fact controverts the statement made in a daily paper, that "unfortunately, without a text to illustrate, 'Phiz' never had half-a-dozen ideas in his head" (!). For many years he was a constant contributor of pictures—figure subjects of a humorous and dramatic character—to the Exhibitions of the British Institution, and of the Society of British Artists. Among his more ambitious efforts was a cartoon of considerable dimensions, representing "A Foraging Party of Cæsar's Forces surprised by the Britons," which appeared as No. 65 at the Westminster Hall Exhibition of 1843. This, notwithstanding the "scratchy" manner of its execution, displayed remarkable skill and abundant energy of design.

At the same gathering another cartoon was attributed to him, of which the energy bordered on caricature; it was named, "Henry II defied by a Welsh Mountaineer."

At one time "Phiz" received an extraordinary commission to reproduce in water-colour all his illustrations to the Novels of DICKENS. The Artist reminded his patron of the magnitude of the undertaking, but the request was persisted in, and the work duly executed.

His love of bracing air induced him to pay frequent visits to the seaside; but on one occasion he lodged in a house not remarkable for its odoriferous nature; and, in order to produce a current of fresh air in his bed-room, he opened door and window, and slept in the draught caused thereby. For many years before his death, he suffered from incipient paralysis, the result, no doubt, of this incautious act, and to which may be attributed his disappearance from the art world some fifteen years ago.

"Phiz," notwithstanding his crippled condition, still worked hard with admirable perseverance, though his difficulties were increased by an injury to his thumb, which compelled him to hold his pencil between the middle and fore fingers. His friends endeavoured to persuade him to draw his pictures on a larger scale, in order that they might be photographed to the required dimensions, but, with one or two exceptions, he refused to act on this suggestion. He gradually lost that facility which characterized his work, and latterly yielded to proposals to illustrate boys' literature of a rather low class.

The time is past, no doubt, which encouraged the method of book-illustration adopted by "Phiz." It has given place to wood-engraving, and multifarious phototypic processes, that, perhaps, are commercially preferable, but from an artistic standpoint much inferior. We must, however, except the wonderful results some wood-engravers have produced from time to time, which etchers, even, cannot hope to excel.

Dr. Edgar Browne describes his father's indifference to the value of his work, or the time and labour bestowed upon it:—"He never understood the art of husbanding or developing his powers,—he never set to work to learn any technical process; when he had a little leisure from 'illustration' work, he used to start a picture 'to get his hand in'—generally taking some unimportant or trivial subject for this purpose. His facility of hand both in large and minute work was something marvellous. At one time, he produced a very remarkable series of sketches in chalk made during a tour in Ireland. They are scattered now, but are as fine as anything he did, and are certainly the best records of a people who have practically vanished. He was astonishingly careless about his work. Hundreds of original designs were thrown into the waste-paper basket; apart from their local interest similar sketches have found willing purchasers of late years."

Like many other artists whose pecuniary reward had not been commensurate with their ability,* he became the recipient of a pension. The kind instrumentality of a few Royal Academicians obtained for him an annual grant which had been previously enjoyed by the late GEORGE CRUIKSHANK.

On the 8th of July, 1882, the death occurred of the famous "Phiz." At the quiet village of Hove, near Brighton, where the last few years of his life were spent, he succumbed in his sixty-seventh year to infirmity rather than old age. Almost forgotten as a man, his productions have remained in our memories, and will continue to do so as long as the works of DICKENS and LEVER are read and appreciated. His remains were interred at the extra-mural Cemetery, Brighton. The funeral was private, the only mourners present being the four sons of the deceased, Dr. Ambler, Mr. George Halse,† and Mr. Robert Harrison.

As admirers of his artistic ability we place this Memoir as a wreath upon his grave.

---

* Publishers frequently availed themselves of his facile pencil, and would instruct him to furnish illustrations for books already in the press, for which he was often inadequately paid.

† The Sculptor, and an old coadjutor on *Once a Week*. He is also the author of *A Salad of Stray Leaves* now in the press, which contains a frontispiece by "Phiz," the last design from his pencil. This he executed under some difficulties, for owing to an attack of rheumatism in his hands, the design—teeming with fancy—had to be made on a large scale, and afterwards reduced by the process of photography.

6 Crescent Place — Margate.
Tuesday.

} given in a former epistle

h'observe.
the address —
when I mentioned
that I managed my
removal without
"any fuss"!
— this style

— Parlour lodgers watch the removal
with intense interest —

CORRESPONDENCE.

The following letters were addressed by the artist-humorist to his son, Mr. Walter G. Browne :—

BLENHEIM CRESCENT,
Sept., Saturday, 3 o'clk. P.M., A.D. 1867.

MY DEAR DR.,

I have nearly bursted my heart out, and proved, that my soul or soles (*I* have two) is'nt—or an't—immortal,--by wearing on 'em out running to and fro after yr. *Balmorals*—Bootless errands! The wretched slave (of awl) has but just brought them! I bristle with wrath! and could welt him!—but—no—I won't—he may want his calf's skin whole, to mend his own *Bad-morals*!!

   *   *   *   *   *

I rush! I fly! to the Gt. W. R. Station! — !!!!

I sink—breathless into the arms of the astounded clerk—point to the boots——

My-mouth faintly whispers "*Wey-mouth* in his pen - adorned *Ear*!!" and—and—"Bless me! where am *I?*"—and, and—I wish—you may get 'em!

   *   *   *   *   *   *

If you visit Portland again, make a note of any peculiarities of spot—convict dress, &c.—as I have a touching bit of horse-y sentiment (!) connected therewith, which will do for *Spg. Gazette.*— I should think you ought to find painty bits—within walking distance—say—right or left ten miles?

   *   *   *   *   *   *

Yrs. affecty.,

DAD.

Sunday.

Really, my dear Walter, I thought you *did* know better than to disturb my devotional frame of mind on this blessed Sabbath morn by forwarding me such a thoroughly worldly and evil-thought-producing thing as a wretched milliner's bill!!!—The wretch must wait—he gorged £5 not long before I left home.—The greediness of some men!!

The Pic. Gall. circular I return—as you may like to enquire about it—the doz. others, "cheap bacon"—"patent teeth and everlasting gums," &c., &c., &c., &c., &c. I shall manure the grounds of Colyton with ——.

I think you might get some background material for coast scenes down here.

Yr. affec. Dad,
II. K. B.

*　　*　　*　　*　　*　　*

69, BLENHEIM CRESCENT, NOTTING HILL,
Saturday.

MY DEAR DOCTOR,

I send the Tenpounder, may it reach you in safety!

The Commander has returned. I sent you a paper containing the important news, which, however, may *not* have reached you, although I don't think it contained any remarks upon the " Hemperors personal appearance," &c., &c., &c.

Tom is in the bosom of the family for a few days.—His Pipe is tuned differently now to what it used to was, for he now declareth that St. John's is "a jolly school!" He seems to get on very well indeed, and has brought home what Dr. Lowe calls a "well-earned prize."

He laments daily over the supposed loss of *4d* invested in a letter to you—from school—as it was directed, he says,—21, Rue *Mussel wine*—I express doubts of its having reached you—and he groans aloud over the Bull's eyes it *would* have bought!——

I am (at *present*) *on* a Sporting Paper—supported by some high and mighty Turf Nobs, but, I fear, like everything I have to do with, now-a-days, it will collapse—for—some of the Proprietors of the Paper are also Shareholders, &c., &c., in the Graphotype Co., so they want to work the two together.—I hate the process—it takes quite four times as long as wood—and I cannot draw and express myself with a nasty little finiking brush, and the result when printed seems to alternate between something all as black as my hat—or as hazy and faint as a worn-out plate.—If on wood, I should like it well enough—as it is —it spoils 4 days a week—leaving little time for anything else. O! I'm a'weary, I'm a'weary! of this illustration business.——

Tom is just off to the R.A., as it is not likely I shall go much before it's close. I will get him to write you a critical description of all the wonderful works in Turps, Varnish, and " Hile."

Yr. affectionate Dad,
II. K. B.

2 *

Monday Morning, 25 m. 40 s. p. 11 A.M.

My Dear Walter

There is a man playing "Home, sweet home" upon the key bugle—it is too much for me—my heart yearneth—I feel I must write just a line or two—especially as it is raining hard—and I don't exactly know what to be at.

*   *   *   *

Splendid effects yesterday evening—sun-set, twilight, crescent moon—stormy clouds—tide out—reflections—dark fishing-craft—very good—quite the thing for you.

There are no people here at present—decidedly nothing Belgravian—chiefly masculines from the Saturday to the Monday sort—it striketh me—a few I think have strayed here from Southend—I saw this sort of thing [*see page 20*] on the Grand Promenade—which looks like it.

There was a great wind yesterday—Boreas had been taking concentrated essence of ginger—It fairly took me off my legs once as I was walking along the cliffs to Broadstairs, luckily for me it blew *off* the sea and I was brought up short by some railings in this wise *see page 22 otherwise* I should (*no doubt*) have been carried across a 5 acre field of *Cloveria Trifolia Browniensis.*—I am glad to say I was also of service to humanity yesterday—I heard the shrill shrieks of a child and a woman's cry for help behind me—I turned and saw there was ot a moment to lose, the wind had caught a poor child—'s hat (and woman's too) and bore it rapidly to the edge of the cliff with my usual agility I bounded over the rails fencing the cliff—and saved yes, saved the child—'s—'at!—another puff and it would have been in the deep, deep sea the blue, the fresh, &c.—Stout mama thanked me politely, and turning to her husband (who, of course, had come up too late to be of any use—those husbands *always* do)—she remarked "That the vind had blown both her and her child's 'at holl' and if she'd know'd it—she wouldn't have brought the young-un hoo."

I dare say humanity is amusing here when the place is full—there seems a good deal of "os" exercise—and basket-carriage driving on Sundays—which is good to behold—this gentleman [*see page 25*] was driving with supreme self-content—having one rein all snug and tight under his pony's tail—luckily the beast did not seem to have any kick in him—so *perhaps* he got safe back to Margate.

*   *   *

Yr. affec. Dad,
H. K. B.

29th Sept. 1868.

My Dear Doctor,

I have sent you a couple of canvasses—if you put little Clara's head on one of them, you will immortalize her and yourself too.

Also therewith you will find a Surplice, and if you will only "hold forth," next Sunday, in the Grande Place of Colyton—I will guarantee to say that the simplicity of yr. vestment and the flowing eloquence of yr. tongue will draw out—(as irresistibly as the Piper did the children) the congregations of the "High" Church and the Conventicles which will—one and all—rush forth for to see and to

hear, and admiringly surround you!—If windy, you might take this
for yr. text—"What went ye forth for to see? A reed shaken by
the wind? &c., &c.

There must have been a splendid *Sea on* at *Sea-ton*, these last few
days, -*tons* of *sea*, eh? As "I took my walk abroad' this morning
—I saw the Serpentine in all its grandeur- and observed several
vessels in distress —some clipper yachts on their beam ends— the
waves were prodigious—great rollers—two especially -one a six
horse fellow—t'other a steamer—crunching and grinding—levelling
and sweeping all before them!

Have you seen the Doge of Colyton yet? or any of the Dog-es?

By all means cultivate the acquaintance of the Doge's kinswoman.
Miss P—— (pray give my love to her)—fac-similed on the stage or in
a novel, she would be a "tremendous hit."

I hope you are not belying the *good* character I have given of you
to the boys—and are doing Elephant, Tiger. and Rhinoceros* to
their perfect satisfaction—though, considering yr. predecessor it
will test your utmost powers, not to be a wretched failure, possibly—
much the same sort of thing—as your attempting to sing a comic
song immediately after the Great Vance!!! Good Night.

Yr. affectionate Dad,

H. K. B.

The following notes have been selected from the unpub-
lished correspondence of "Phiz" with CHARLES DICKENS:—

MY DEAR DICKENS,

I have just got one boot on, intending to come round
to you, but you have done me out of a capital excuse to myself
for idling away this fine morning.—I quite forgot to answer your
note, and Mr. Macrone's book has not been very vividly present
to my memory for some time past. I think by the beginning of next
(week) or the middle (*certain*) I shall have done the plates, but in the
scraps of copy that I have I can see but *one good* subject, so if you
know of another pray send it me. I should like "Malcolm" again.
if you can spare him.

Believe me,

Yours very truly,

HABLOT K. BROWNE.

Charles Dickens, Esq.

—

Sunday, Sept.

MY DEAR DICKENS,

Can you conveniently send me the subject or subjects for
next week by Thursday or Friday? as I wish, if practicable,
to start for Brussels by the Sunday's boat—a word in reply will oblige,

Yours truly,

HABLOT K. BROWNE.

Charles Dickens, Esq.

P.S.—Upon second thoughts I send you the enclosed epistle

* A favourite game with the children.

(if you read it, you will find out why)—the writer thereof is "Harry Lorrequer," alias "Charles O'Malley"—to whose house I am going.

H. K. B.

P.S. Second—A fortnight's furlough would suit me better than a week, if it could be managed, as I should like to return by Holland.

MY DEAR DICKENS,

I am sorry I cannot have a touch at battledore with you to-day, being already booked for this evening—but I will give you a call to-morrow *after church*, and take my chance of finding you at home.

Yours very sincerely,
HABLOT K BROWNE.

Charles Dickens, Esq.

33, HOWLAND STREET.

MY DEAR DICKENS,

I shall be most happy to remember not to forget the 10th April, and, let me express a *disinterested* wish, that having completed and established one "Shop"* in an "extensive line of business," you will go on increasing and multiplying such like establishments in number and prosperity till you become a Dick Whittington of a merchant, with pockets distended to most Brobdignag dimensions.

Believe me,
Yours very truly,
HABLOT K. BROWNE.

Charles Dickens, Esq.

I return you the Riots with many thanks.

* *The Old Curiosity Shop.*

Sunday Morning.

My Dear Dickens,

Will you give me some notion of the sort of design you wish for the frontispiece to second vol. of *Clock?*[*] Cattermole being put *hors de combat* — Chapman with a careworn face (if you can picture that) brings me the block at the eleventh hour, and requires it finished by Wednesday. Now as I have two others to complete in the meantime — something nice and *light* would be best adapted to my *palette*, and prevent an excess of perspiration in the relays of wood-cutters. You shall have the others to criticise on Tuesday.

Yours very truly.
HABLOT K. BROWNE.

Charles Dickens, Esq.

How are Mrs. Dickens and the "Infant?"

A LIST OF THE PRINCIPAL WORKS ILLUSTRATED
BY "PHIZ."

To enumerate all the works illustrated by "Phiz" would be a next to impossible task, for "their name is legion." No artist was so popular or so prolific as a book-illustrator, with the exception, perhaps, of George Cruikshank. It may fairly be questioned whether the works of Charles Dickens, with which the name of "Phiz" is most intimately associated in our minds, would have achieved such notoriety without the aid of the etching needle so ably wielded. Mr. John Hollingshead, in his essay on Dickens, says :—

"The greater the value of a book as a literary production, the more will the circle of its influence usually be narrowed. The very shape, aspect, and garments of the ideal creatures who move through its pages, even when drawn by the pen of the first master of fiction in the land, will be faint and confused to the blunter perception of the general reader, unless aided by the attendant pencil of the illustrative artist. For the sharp, clear images of Mr. Pickwick, with the spectacles, gaiters, and low crowned hat—of Sam Weller, with the striped waistcoat and the artful leer—of Mr. Winkle, with the sporting costume and the foolish expression—more persons are indebted to the caricaturist, than to the faultless descriptive passages of the great creative mind that called the amusing puppets into existence."

It was not the fame of Dickens only that was enhanced by "Phiz," for the numerous illustrations in the works of Charles Lever, Harrison Ainsworth, the brothers Mayhew,

---

[*] *Master Humphrey's Clock.*

and a host of minor novelists were executed by his unwearied hand. It was Dickens, however, who introduced him to public notice, in a pamphlet, now very scarce, entitled *Sunday under Three Heads*, embellished with four delicately executed engravings drawn by "H. K. B."

It was his succession to Seymour as the illustrator of the *Pickwick Papers*, that really excited public interest in the youthful artist, who created, pictorially, the second hero in the work, the inimitable Samuel Weller. Those who are familiar with the original edition of the *Pickwick Papers* will remember with some amusement, the artist's introduction of the indefatigable "Boots," as represented in the yard of the "White Hart" Inn, Borough. The identical Inn exists at the present day. "Mr. Pickwick in the Pound" is another amusing plate, where the laughing, jeering crowd of spectators crowned by a jubilant and juvenile chimney sweeper, the braying of a jackass in the ears of the astonished hero, who sits somewhat uncomfortably in a wheelbarrow, are incidents so cleverly depicted as to excite unqualified admiration. "Mr. Pickwick Slides" is another truly artistic production. The delicate execution of the extreme distance where is seen a manor house of the olden time nestling amongst the trees, and a farmyard hard by, leaves nothing to be desired. Mr. Sala somewhat harshly criticises the illustrations in this work, which, he says, "were exceedingly humorous, but vilely drawn. The amazing success of his author seems, however, to have spurred the artist to sedulous study, and to have conduced in a remarkable degree towards the development of his faculties. A surprising improvement was visible in the frontispieces to the completed volumes* of *Pickwick*." Undoubtedly faults exist, but to characterize the illustrations as "vile," seems too severe a term, for after all, the exaggerated types of face, form, and feature, do but harmonize with the somewhat exaggerated descriptions of them by the author. This defect, if such it can be called, was remedied considerably in his later productions.

In 1837, "Phiz" accompanied Dickens into Yorkshire, there to gather material for *Nicholas Nickleby*, a work which exposes the tyranny practised by some schoolmasters on their helpless pupils. In this book, published in 1839, is

---

* The *Pickwick Papers* were issued in *one* volume, and with *one* frontispiece.

presented to us the despicable "Squeers," which type of brute in human form was so successfully realized by both Author and Artist, that the indignation of innumerable Yorkshire pedagogues was raised to threats of legal proceedings, for traducing their characters, one of them actually stating that "he remembered being waited on last January twelvemonth by two gentlemen, one of whom held him in conversation while the other took his likeness." The most familiar representation of "Squeers" is seen in the second plate, where he stands sharpening his pen, and is timorously approached by the stout father of two wizen-faced boys who are about to become his pupils. The face of the schoolmaster, in which are combined hypocrisy and cruelty, and the expression of sympathy for the new comers exhibited by the boy on the trunk, are worthy of the closest inspection. The effect of the school treatment at Dotheboy's Hall is visible in the illustration where "The Internal Economy" is depicted. Here we see the starveling lads during and after the "internal" application of superabundant doses of brimstone and treacle, administered by Squeers' worthy partner. The eighth plate happily depicts the wild excitement of the pupils when "Nicholas astonishes Mr. Squeers and family" by making a furious attack on the former with the cane; as well as "The breaking-up at Dotheboy's Hall," where the boys revenge themselves on their former tormentors. There are two more etchings in this volume especially remarkable as artistic productions, viz., "Mr. and Mrs. Mantalini in Ralph Nickleby's Office," where the expression of an intent listener on the face of Ralph, and of horror on that of Mantalini, is capitally rendered; and the plate

entitled "The Recognition," which shows poor Smike in the act of rising from a couch of sickness as he recognizes "Broker," who had conveyed him as a child to school.

Master Humphrey's Clock, written in 1840-1, includes the stories of the *Old Curiosity Shop* and *Barnaby Rudge* which have been happily termed "two unequalled twin fictions upon one stem." The illustrations were drawn on wood by H. K. Browne and George Cattermole, and the former created, pictorially, Little Nell, Mrs. Jarley, Quilp, Dick Swiveller, the Marchioness, Sally Brass, and her brother Sampson. "Phiz" revelled in wild fun in the vignettes relating to the devilries of Mr. Daniel Quilp and the humours of Codlin and Short, and of Mrs. Jarley's waxwork show. His "Marchioness" was a distinct comic creation; but in the weird waterscape, showing the corpse of Quilp washed ashore, he sketched a vista of riparian scenery which, in its desolate breadth and loneliness, has not since, perhaps, been equalled, save in the amazing suggestive Thames etchings of Mr. James Whistler. To be sure, Hablot Browne was stimulated to excellence during the continuance of the *Old Curiosity Shop* by the friendly rivalry of the famous water-colour painter, George Cattermole, who drew the charming vignettes of the quaint old cottages and school-house and church of the village where "Little Nell" died. In *Barnaby Rudge*, however, Hablot Browne had things graphic his own way, and again towards the close he manifested genuine tragic power. His "Barnaby with the Raven" is lovely in its picturesque grace.* When the first cheap series of this work was published, plates by H. K. Browne were issued, which are now so scarce, that they are often catalogued at eight or ten times their original price.

Two years after the visit of Dickens to America in 1842, *Martin Chuzzlewit* was published, the illustrations to which excel in vigour all the previous efforts of "Phiz." Here we are brought face to face, in a pictorial sense, with the hypocrite, Mr. Pecksniff, the *abstemious* Mrs. Gamp and her bosom friend, Betsy Prig, simple Tom Pinch and his charming sister, Ruth. The frontispiece is a most ambitious work, but none the less successful, for "Phiz" has represented, in the space of a few square inches, all the leading events, humorous and pathetic, described in the novel. In the illustration where Mark Tapley is seen starting from his native village for London, "Phiz" exhibits his sense

* *The Daily Telegraph*, July 11th, 1882.

of the picturesque in the old gables and dormers of the cottages which form the background. The plate, "Mr. Pecksniff on his Mission," is full of interest, and gives us an insight into the character of Kingsgate Street, Holborn, at that time. The female neighbours of Mrs. Gamp, the midwife, flock round Pecksniff, commiserating with him on his supposed domestic cares, and advising him to "knock at the winder, Sir; knock at the winder. Lord bless you, don't lose no more time than you can help—knock at the winder!"

But the etching in *Chuzzlewit* which most strikes the reader as a ludicrous conception, is that where "Mrs. Gamp propoges a toast." Here he has admirably illustrated the text, wherein is described, with other details of a droll character, how some rusty gowns and other articles of that lady's wardrobe depended from the bed-posts; and "these had so adapted themselves by long usage to her figure, that more than one impatient husband, coming in precipitately, at about the time of twilight, had been for an instant stricken dumb by the supposed discovery that Mrs. Gamp had hanged herself." In the background of the picture are represented these indispensable articles of dress, while at the table sit, in friendly chat, Mrs. Gamp and Betsy.

"Betsy," said Mrs. Gamp, filling her own glass and passing the tea-pot, "I will now propoge a toast. My frequent pardner, Betsy Prig!"

"Which, altering the name to Sairah Gamp; I drink," said Mrs. Prig, "with love and tenderness."

In 1846, *Dombey and Son* commenced, with forty illustrations by "Phiz." The frontispiece is similar in design to that of *Chuzzlewit*, introducing the principal characters and events in the novel. The austere and pompous (not to say selfish) Mr. Dombey, whom "Phiz" had great difficulty in realizing to the author's satisfaction,* is introduced in many of the plates, although the artist has somewhat failed in preserving the same type of face throughout. He has succeeded better with the genial Captain Cuttle. Little Paul, as he sits in his diminutive arm-chair, contrasts most favourably in his childish innocence, with the grim Mrs. Pipchin, whose Ogress-like character is strongly marked. The scene in which Mr. Dombey introduces his daughter Florence to Mrs. Skewton, is one of the most successful in the book, and contains the *best* type of Dombey. Here also, the face of Florence is truly pretty, and the

* See illustration facing page 11.

artist has well portrayed the handsome but vindictive Edith denouncing Carker for his treachery. A very effective etching entitled, "On the Dark Road," represents the flight of the enraged and disappointed libertine. The horses are being urged on their mad career by the whip and spurs of a postilion, under the dark sky with a glimmer of light in the horizon caused by the rising sun. The artist at this time essayed a process of working on plates over which a half-tint had been previously laid by means of a ruling-machine, and in which the "high-lights" were afterwards "stopped out," and the "whites" "burnished out." He frequently availed himself of these ready means of producing effect. Full-length portraits of the principal characters in *Dombey*, which were issued as additional plates by "Phiz," are now very scarce.

David Copperfield (1850), with forty illustrations, was the next venture, but was not so much an artistic as a literary success. A favourite character in it of course, is Micawber, a kindly caricature of the Author's father, the realization of whom, by Browne, obtained the hearty approval of Dickens.

The most characteristic and, perhaps, most successful work of "Phiz" is to be seen in the illustrations to *Bleak House*. A view of the "House" itself forms the subject of the frontispiece. "The Ghost's Walk," the "Drawing-room at Chesney Wold," "Tom All-alone's," and the gateway leading to the burial ground where Lady Dedlock has fallen lifeless, are instances where the artist has obtained some fine effects by the "ruled-plate" process. A writer in *The Daily Telegraph*, of July 11th, 1882, speaks somewhat disparagingly of these illustrations, but *The Academy* of a few days later, in the following remarks, thus demurs to his criticism:—

"In the *Bleak House* illustrations hardly anything is wrong; there is no shortcoming. Not only is the comic side, the even fussily comic, such as 'the young man of the name of Guppy,' understood and rendered well, but the dignified beauty of old country-house architecture, or the architecture of the chambers of our inns-of-court is conveyed in brief touches; and there is apparent everywhere that element of terrible suggestiveness which made not only the art of Hablot Browne, but the art of Charles Dickens himself, in this story of *Bleak House*, recall the imaginative purpose of the art of Méryon. What can be more impressive in connection with the story—nay, even independently of the story—than the illustration of Mr. Tulkinghorn's chambers in gloom; than the illustration of the staircase at Dedlock's own house, with the placard of the reward for the discovery of the murderer; than that of Tom All Alone's; the dark, foul darkness of the burial ground shown under scanty lamplight, and the special spot where lay the man who 'wos very good to me—he wos!'? And then again, 'the Ghost's Walk,' and once more the burial ground, with the woman's body—Lady Dedlock's—now close against its gate. Of course it would be possible to find fault with these things, but they have nothing of the vice of tameness—they deliver their message effectually.

It is not their business to be faultless; it is their business to impress."

A very successful rendering of character in *Bleak House* is that of Harold Skimpole, whose prototype was Leigh Hunt, an intimate friend of the Novelist, who, by his unintentional disregard for the feelings of Hunt in caricaturing his peculiarities, nearly severed that friendship. Again, there is intense humour in the illustration facetiously styled, "In re Guppy, extraordinary proceeding." The love-sick Guppy is seen in a kneeling posture, while declaring to Miss Summerson the burning passion that consumes him. The expression on the face of the young lady shows that she is more amused than flattered by his preference.

In *Little Dorrit* (1855-7) the experience gained by both Author and Artist during their tour of the London prisons, stood them in good stead, for here the Marshalsea is fully described, the type of a debtor's jail. The first illustration represents the interior of a French prison, in which are incarcerated Monsieur Rigand and Signor John Baptist. The effect of deep gloom in the cell is produced by the "ruled-plate" method, and is quite Rembrandt-like. In contrast with this, the illustration of "The Ferry," is a delightful country aspect, with trees and winding river ; and another plate entitled "Floating away," an evening scene, the moon rising behind the trees, is quite romantic. The old house in the last picture but one—"Damocles,"—again shows Browne's appreciation of the picturesque architecture of bygone times, in the effect of light from the setting sun as it falls upon the house front, throwing into relief the quaint old carvings of door and window.

The last work illustrated by "Phiz" for Dickens was *The Tale of Two Cities* (1859), containing sixteen etchings full of vigour, as the character of the story justifies.

For some reason, at this time, a rupture was caused between author and artist,* which resulted in the engagement of Mr. Marcus Stone and Mr. Luke Fildes as illustrators of *Our Mutual Friend* and *Edwin Drood*. These accomplished painters avoided the old system of caricature, the old, forced humour ; but it is certain that their designs are less intimately associated with the persons in the stories they illustrated than those of "Phiz" with the earlier and more popular works of Dickens.

Having devoted the larger portion of the space at our disposal to a description of the most famous productions of Browne's pencil, which are prominent in the original editions of the Novels of Charles Dickens, we can but briefly enumerate the plates he etched for Lever, Ainsworth, and others.

In Charles Lever's *Harry Lorrequer* (1839) and *Charles O'Malley* (1841), the uproarious mirth and jollity of Irish military life is well portrayed by the needle of the artist. "The last night in Trinity" in the latter work, is an ex-

* If the following statement, made in the *Frankfurt Zeitung*, can be credited, any feeling of enmity that existed between them had long since died out :—"Just after the death of Charles Dickens, 'Phiz' was considerably affected by the mere mention of the name of that illustrious novelist, which seemed to stir up in his breast feelings of regret at losing such a friend."

ample of this, wherein is seen the worthy Doctor perched on a table, surrounded by a batch of Irish dragoons, and being elevated by an explosion of combustibles. The horses in the illustrations are admirably drawn.

In *Jack Hinton* (1842) the artist shows remarkable force in depicting the death of Shaun, and has well realized the humour of "Corney's Combat with the Cossack."

Tom Burke of Ours (1844) contains forty-four illustrations by "Phiz," many of which represent the scenes connected with the battles of Austerlitz, &c., during the reign of the great Napoleon. Most especially noticeable is the scene in a court of justice, with "Darby in the Chair;" the face of that hero with an expression apparently abashed, but really full of roguishness, as he gazes at the counsel, is one of the most successful of Browne's efforts.

The O'Donoghue (1845), has twenty-six illustrations, most of which are well conceived. The falling body of a man in the frontispiece is a remarkable drawing. The girlish figure of Kate O'Donoghue, as she bends over the form of her heart-broken brother Herbert, is well depicted.

St. Patrick's Eve (1845), with four etchings and several woodcuts. The most remarkable of the former is "The Cholera Hut."

The Knight of Gwynne (1847), with forty illustrations.

Roland Cashel (1850), with forty illustrations.

The Daltons (1852), with forty-eight illustrations.

The Dodd Family Abroad (1854), with forty illustrations. The shrewd simplicity of Kenny Dodd is well delineated.

The Martins of Cro' Martin (1856), with forty illustrations.

Davenport Dunn (1859), with forty-four illustrations.

One of Them (1861), with thirty illustrations.

Barrington (1863), with twenty-six illustrations.

Luttrell of Arran (1865), with thirty-two illustrations.

The following works of W. Harrison Ainsworth contain etchings and woodcuts by "Phiz:"—

Revelations of London, published about 1845, but never completed, has an illustration which represents a tumble-down house in Vauxhall Road, which is almost Rembrandt-like in its power. The artist was about thirty years of age when he executed this.

Old St. Paul's (1847), contains only two plates by "Phiz," but *The Spendthrift* (1857), *Mervyn Clitheroe*, and *Crichton* were wholly illustrated by him.

32

SOME MISCELLANEOUS WORKS ILLUSTRATED BY "PHIZ."

A Paper: of Tobacco, &c., by Joseph Fume (1839). With six plates by "Phiz." *Fiddle Faddle's Sentimental Tour, in search of the Amusing, Picturesque, and Agreeable* (1845). *The Union Magazine.* Vol. I (1846). Containing three plates by "Phiz." *The Illuminated Magazine.* Conducted by Douglas Jerrold (1843-5), with woodcut illustrations by Leech, "Phiz" (H. K. Browne), and others. *Fanny, the little Milliner, or the Rich and the Poor* (1846), illustrated by "Phiz" and Onwhyn. *Wits and Beaux of Society. Sketches of Cantabs, by John Smith (of Smith Hall), Gent.* (1850). *The Cambridge Freshman.* With woodcut illustrations. *Paved with Gold, or Romance and Reality of the London Streets,* by Augustus Mayhew (1858). *A Medical, Moral, and Christian Dissection of Teetotalism by Democritus* (1846). *New Sporting Magazine* (1839). *The Pottleton Legacy,* by Albert Smith. *Christmas Day, and how it was spent by four persons in the house of Fograss, Fograss, Mowton, and Snorton, bankers,* by C. Le Ros (1854). *Home Pictures* (Durtin & Co., 1856). A series of seven charming and characteristic plates. *Dame Perkins and her Grey Mare, or the Mount for Market,* by L. Meadows (1866). With coloured illustrations. *H. B.'s Schoolboy Days. Illustrations of the Five Senses. Adventures of Sir Guy de Guy,* by George Halse. *The Baddington Peerage,* by G. A. Sala (published in *The Illustrated Times*). In addition to these may be added an illustrated edition of Byron's works, the "Abbotsford" edition of Sir Walter Scott's Novels, besides numerous cuts in *The Sporting Gazette, The Illustrated Times,* the early volumes of *Once a Week,* and the Comic Papers.

(SOME SIGNATURES ADOPTED BY H. K. BROWNE.)

www.ingramcontent.com/pod-product-compliance
Lightning Source LLC
Chambersburg PA
CBHW031322280626
47169CB00019B/2786